AFTER

HAPPILY EVER AFTER

The Fairy Godmother
Takes a Break

First published in the United States in 2009
by Stone Arch Books
151 Good Counsel Drive, P.O. Box 669
Mankato, Minnesota 56002
www.stonearchbooks.com

First published by Orchard Books, a division of Hachette Children's Books.
338 Euston Road, London NW1 3BH, United Kingdom

Library of Congress Cataloging-in-Publication Data
Bradman, Tony.
    The Fairy Godmother Takes a Break / by Tony Bradman; illustrated by
Sarah Warburton.
    p. cm. — (After Happily Ever After)
    ISBN 978-1-4342-1302-0 (library binding)
    [1. Fairy godmothers—Fiction.] I. Warburton, Sarah, ill. II. Title.
PZ7.B7275Fai 2009
[Fic]—dc22   2008031829

Summary: The Fairy Godmother is tired of helping everyone else live happily
ever after. Nobody ever thanks her, and she's had enough! Find out if the
fairy godmother can really quit her job.

Creative Director: Heather Kindseth
Graphic Designer: Emily Harris

1 2 3 4 5 6 14 13 12 11 10 09

Printed in the United States of America

AFTER HAPPILY EVER AFTER

The Fairy Godmother Takes a Break

by Tony Bradman
illustrated by Sarah Warburton

STONE ARCH BOOKS
www.stonearchbooks.com

So the Fairy Godmother granted
wish after wish and
everyone she helped lived
happily ever after.
And then …

Deep in the forest there stands a little cottage. In that cottage is a cozy bedroom, where somebody's alarm clock is about to go off.

BEEP-BEEP-BEEP! BEEP-BEEP-BEEP! BEEP-BEEP-BEEP!

"Oh no!" groaned the Fairy Godmother.
"It can't possibly be time to get up already.
I feel like I've only just gone to bed."

"Sorry, dear," said her husband, Mr. Fairy Godmother. "I set the alarm for earlier than usual. I think it could be a very busy day."

"So what's new?" muttered the Fairy Godmother. She pulled the covers over her head. "Busy, busy, busy. I never get a second to myself, Mr. F.G.!"

"Oh well, never mind," said Mr. F.G. "I'll go and put the kettle on."

The Fairy Godmother kept muttering under the covers.

She muttered in the shower, and while she got dressed too. She was still muttering when she sat down at the kitchen table. Mr. F.G. put a nice cup of tea in front of her.

"Nobody ever thanks me, either," she said.

"Take Cinderella, for instance. I spent a whole week running around for her, putting spells on rats and mice and pumpkins. And have I heard from her since?"

"Well, dear," said Mr. F.G., "that's probably because . . ."

"I'm tired of granting wishes," the Fairy Godmother muttered, interrupting him. "Anyway, where will I be waving my wand today?"

"I'll find out," said Mr. F.G. "I just need to switch on the computer."

Soon Mr. F.G. was sitting before a large, glowing screen. He worked as his wife's personal assistant, and he had a special, magic computer that only accepted one kind of message: wish-mails.

RECEIVING MESSAGES...

Whenever someone in the forest made a wish, it instantly arrived on the screen with a PING!

Mr. F.G. tapped the keyboard, and the wish-mails started to come in. There were more than usual, and the screen quickly filled up.

"That's it!" said the Fairy Godmother.
"I've had enough. I quit. I resign.

And just to make it absolutely official . . ."

She held up her magic wand and
snapped it in half. Mr. F.G. winced.

"Oh dear," said Mr. F.G. "Would you like another cup of tea?"

"No thanks," said the Fairy Godmother. "I'd rather have a vacation!"

Mr. F.G. sighed again, but he called Fairy Tale Vacations and arranged everything.

The next morning they flew out of Forest Airport. A few hours later they arrived at Club Enchantment, their vacation destination.

"Ah, this is the life," said the Fairy
Godmother as Mr. F.G. unpacked their
suitcases. "Sun, sea, and sand! I can feel
myself relaxing already."

Mr. and Mrs. F.G. spent the day
swimming, sunbathing, and reading books.

In the evening they had dinner at
The Magic Spoon, Club Enchantment's
best restaurant.

The band was really cool, and the food
was a thousand times better than Mr. F.G.'s
cooking.

But the Fairy Godmother didn't seem too happy.

"Those dwarves over there are staring at me," she whispered.

"Oh no, I don't think they are, dear," murmured Mr. F.G., who was diving into his dinner. "This lobster is terrific. You really should try some."

"They are staring at me, and I don't like it," the Fairy Godmother said. "And I'm NOT going to put up with it, either. Come on, we're leaving!"

"B-b-but . . ." Mr. F.G. sputtered. Then he sighed, paid the bill, and followed his wife, looking longingly at the lovely lobster he was leaving behind.

The next morning they went to the
beach again. Mr. F.G. had just got to a
good part in his book when the Fairy
Godmother poked him in the ribs.

"Psst!" she hissed at him. "Somebody
else is staring at me now."

"Calm down, dear," said Mr. F.G.,
looking up. "I don't think anyone . . .
actually, you're right. He is staring at you,
isn't he? How strange."

A young troll in swimming trunks couldn't
take his eyes off the Fairy Godmother.

And as they watched him, he smiled shyly and waved. Then he said something to a family of elves nearby and pointed at her. Soon they were smiling at her too. And so was everyone else on the beach!

"You realize what this means, don't you?" the Fairy Godmother hissed to Mr. F.G. from the corner of her mouth. "They all know who I am!"

"Oh, of course!" said Mr. F.G. "But that's no surprise. You've helped so many people, dear. There are bound to be some here who recognize you."

"Next they'll be asking me to grant wishes," she said. "And you know I won't get a word of thanks. Come on—we're leaving!"

"Yes, dear," murmured Mr. F.G., closing his book with a deep sigh.

That evening they didn't go to The Magic Spoon, but to another restaurant instead. It wasn't as good.

The Fairy Godmother wore dark glasses and a scarf. She didn't take them off even when she was eating. But people still stared at her and smiled and waved.

Then, the next day on the beach, the
Fairy Godmother suddenly froze.

"Oh no," she whispered to Mr. F.G.,
panic in her voice. "Don't look now, but I
think that princess is coming over to talk
to me. Come on, we're . . ."

"I know, I know," muttered Mr. F.G.
"We're leaving."

The Fairy Godmother hurried off, and Mr. F.G. hurried behind her carrying their bags, with the princess in hot pursuit.

In the end, the Fairy Godmother and Mr. F.G. were practically running, but the princess caught up with them.

"Please, wait!" she called out. "I'm sorry, but I simply had to make sure it was you. I would never, ever forgive myself if I missed this chance."

"Sorry! Can't stop!" said the Fairy
Godmother. "Come along, dear!"

"I want to say thank you for everything
you did for me," said the princess.

"I'm Cinderella, in case you'd forgotten. You totally changed my life."

"Did I really?" said the Fairy Godmother, peering at the princess for a second, then smiling. "Yes, I remember you now. Well, how are things?"

Cinderella told the Fairy Godmother all about her new life with Prince Charming. Cinders also said she would have thanked her before, but didn't have any way of getting in touch with her.

As they talked, lots more people came up to the Fairy Godmother and said exactly the same thing.

"Anyway, enjoy the rest of your vacation," said Cinders. The Fairy Godmother beamed at her.

"Although I bet you can't wait to go home and start helping people again. How wonderful to have a job like yours. Goodbye!" said Cinders.

The Fairy Godmother's smile vanished, and suddenly she looked upset. And by the time she and Mr. F.G. were back in their room, she was in tears.

"Cinderella is right," she moaned. "It is a wonderful job, and I've thrown it away. Why didn't you tell me no one knows how to send me any thanks?"

"I did try," said Mr. F.G. "Anyway, I'm sure that's a problem I can solve. You need to get out a bit more, too, maybe do some follow-up visits."

"Follow-ups to what?" she wailed. "I won't be able to grant wishes any more. I broke my wand, remember? Although now I wish that I hadn't."

"Well, your wish is granted," said Mr. F.G., smiling. He opened one of their suitcases and pulled out her wand. "Sort of, anyway. I mended it before we left home. And though I say so myself, it's almost as good as new."

The Fairy Godmother looked at it in
amazement and hugged him.

They enjoyed the rest of their vacation.
And even though there were loads of wish-
mails waiting for them when they got
home, the Fairy Godmother didn't mind.

In fact, she was eager to get back to work now that she felt more appreciated. Mr. F.G. liked having the cottage to himself too.

So the Fairy Godmother and Mr. F.G.
and just about everyone in the forest who
made a wish lived **HAPPILY EVER AFTER!**

THE END

ABOUT THE AUTHOR

Tony Bradman writes for children of all ages.
He is particularly well known for his top-selling
Dilly the Dinosaur series. His other titles include
the Happily Ever After series, The Orchard Book
of Heroes and Villains, and The Orchard Book of
Swords, Sorcerers, and Superheroes. Tony lives in
South East London.

ABOUT THE ILLUSTRATOR

Sarah Warburton is a rising star in children's
books. She is the illustrator of the Rumblewick
series, which has been very well received at an
international level. The series spans across both
picture books and fiction. She has also illustrated
nonfiction titles and the Happily Ever After series.
She lives in Bristol, England, with her young baby
and husband.

GLOSSARY

assistant (uh-SISS-tuhnt)—a person who helps another person

mended (MEND-id)—fixed

muttered (MUHT-urd)—to speak in a low, unclear way

peering (PIHR-ing)—looking closely at something or someone

pursuit—(PUR-soot)—the act of chasing or following somone

recognize (REK-uhg-nize)—to know and remember from before

relaxing (ri-LAKS-ing)—becoming less tense

spells (spels)—a word or words that may have magic powers

sunbathing (SUHN-bayth-ing)—to lay out in the sun

vanished (VAN-ishd)—disappeared

DISCUSSION QUESTIONS

1. The Fairy Godmother's job is to grant wishes. If you were the Fairy Godmother, who would you grant three wishes to and why?

2. When the Fairy Godmother doesn't feel appreciated, she quits her job. Discuss a time when you felt underappreciated.

3. The Fairy Godmother is a celebrity. She is recognized wherever she goes. Many celebrities don't have any privacy. What do you think it feels like to never have privacy?

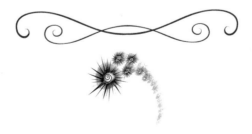

WRITING PROMPTS

1. The Fairy Godmother picked a relaxing vacation on the beach. If you could go anywhere in the world, where would it be? Write a paragraph describing where you would go and whom you would invite.

2. The Fairy Godmother is getting so many wish-mails that she needs another personal assistant. Write an ad for the newspaper describing the type of assistant the Fairy Godmother needs.

3. The Fairy Godmother is a well-known celebrity. Pretend you are the president of her fan club. Write the Fairy Godmother a letter from her number one fan.

Before there was **HAPPILY EVER AFTER,**
there was **ONCE UPON A TIME …**

Read the **ORIGINAL** fairy tales in **NEW** graphic novel retellings.

INTERNET SITES

Do you want to know more about subjects related to this book? Or are you interested in learning about other topics? Then check out FactHound, a fun, easy way to find Internet sites.

Our investigative staff has already sniffed out great sites for you!

Here's how to use FactHound:

1. Visit *www.facthound.com*

2. Select your grade level.

3. To learn more about subjects related to this book, type in the book's ISBN number: **1434213021**.

4. Click the Fetch It button.

FactHound will fetch the best Internet sites for you!